THE OFFICIAL Harry Potter HOW TO DRAW

SCHOLASTIC INC.

Scholastic Inc., 557 Broadway, New York, NY 10012 • Scholastic UK Ltd., 1 London Bridge, London, SE1 9BG
Scholastic LTD, Unit 89E, Lagan Road, Dublin Industrial Estate, Glasnevin, Dublin 11

ISBN 978-1-339-03231-3

10 9 8 7 6 5 4 3 2 1   24 25 26 27 28

Printed in China   38

First printing 2024

Written by **Isa Gouache**
Additional Illlustrations by **Violet Tobacco**
Book design by **Salena Mahina** and **Elliane Mellet**
Edited by **Samantha Swank**

TABLE of CONTENTS

BEGINNER

HARRY'S GLASSES 8
BROOM 9
WAND 11
THE GOLDEN SNITCH 13
SORTING HAT 15

SWORD OF GRYFFINDOR 18
LUNA'S SPECTRESPECS 20
TIME-TURNER 23
CHOCOLATE FROG BOX 26

INTERMEDIATE

ARAGOG 28
CROOKSHANKS 31
HEDWIG 34
HIPPOGRIFF 38
THESTRAL 41
DOBBY 44

HOWLER 47
MONSTER BOOK OF MONSTERS 50
GRYFFINDOR CREST 54
SLYTHERIN CREST 58
RAVENCLAW CREST 60
HUFFLEPUFF CREST 62

ADVANCED

HARRY POTTER 65
RON WEASLEY 68
HERMIONE GRANGER 71
DRACO MALFOY 74
LUNA LOVEGOOD 77

ALBUS DUMBLEDORE 80
HOGWARTS EXPRESS 83
HOGWARTS CREST 86
HOGWARTS CASTLE 89
THE KNIGHT BUS 93

WELCOME TO THE MAGICAL WORLD OF DRAWING!

Ready to learn everything there is to know about drawing Harry Potter, his friends, and the magical objects and creatures that make up the films of the Wizarding World? This book will show you how—step by step, and one drawing at a time. So, gather up your drawing supplies. And get ready to have fun!

WHAT YOU'LL NEED:

- A pencil
- An eraser
- Paper

YOU MAY ALSO WANT:

- Scrap paper (for practice)
- Nicer paper (for your final drawing)
- A thin black marker
- Colored pencils, markers, or paints
- A straightedge or ruler
- A compass or something with a round base like a cup
- A snack!

ALL ABOUT THIS BOOK

The drawings in this book are split into three levels—beginner, intermediate, and advanced. The drawings start off basic and get more challenging as you go. But you may find an advanced drawing kind of easy or a beginner drawing really hard. That's okay! Go at your own pace. There are plenty of drawing tips throughout this book to help you along the way.

7 Draw a curved line inside the top of the hat's brim to make it look 3-D. Then draw a similar line inside the bottom of the hat's opening.

8 Finish up by filling in the eyes, mouth, and opening in the brim. Which character will you sort first?

SWORD OF GRYFFINDOR

This sword has the ability to do the nearly impossible: destroy Lord Voldemort's horcruxes. Harry also uses it to defeat a Basilisk in the second film! Drawing the design on the sword's hilt (or handle) may feel challenging, but you can take it slow and break the design down into simple shapes. Try tracing it on scrap paper first to get a feel for where the lines go. Tracing is a great way to practice!

1 Draw two long, skinny rectangles that crisscross. The horizontal rectangle should be longer than the vertical rectangle.

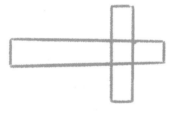

2 To draw the shape of the sword's handle, first look for the basic shapes, like circles, ovals, and squares. Draw all the shapes you see in the handle, then connect them with curved lines.

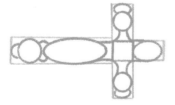

3 Trace an outline around the shapes you drew in step two. Then erase all the lines inside the outline as well as the rectangles from step one.

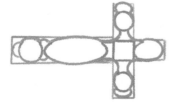

4 There are rubies set into the sword's handle. Use circles and ovals to draw them inside the handle shape from step three.

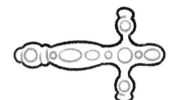

5 Draw two long lines for the sword's blade, getting a little closer together as you go out. Then add a "V" connecting them for the sharp point.

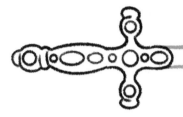

6 Turn your paper on its side. Then write the name "Godric Gryffindor" on the sword's blade. The letters should be stacked on top of each other instead of side to side.

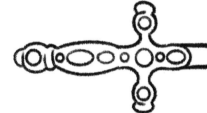

7 Are you feeling as powerful as this magical sword? Then color in the rubies Gryffindor red and the rest of the sword in shiny silver!

LUNA'S SPECTRESPECS

Luna Lovegood uses her Spectrespecs to see Wrackspurts, invisible floating creatures that make the brain go fuzzy. This drawing uses guidelines to help you see where to draw the edges of these colorful spectacles. Feeling fuzzy? Guidelines may be invisible in the final drawing but they can help you visualize the steps you need to take to get there!

1 Start by drawing a circle inside a circle just like you did for Harry's glasses. Then draw another circle inside a circle right next to it.

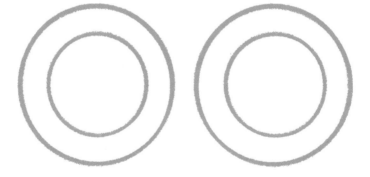

2 How far out do you want the edges of the Spectrespecs to go? Once you know, draw a curved guideline outside each of the larger circles. You'll need these guidelines in the next step!

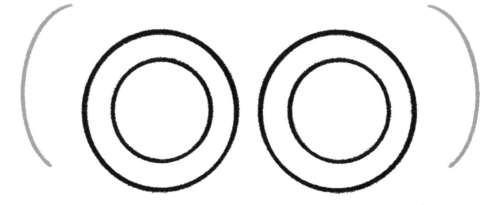

3 On the outside edge of each circle, draw a wavy line with fives bumps to create the sides of the Spectrespecs. The top of each bump should hit the guidelines you drew in step two.

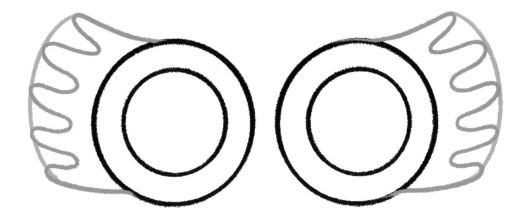

4 Connect the two bigger circles with two curved lines. Then clean up your drawing and erase any lines you don't need—including the guidelines!

5 Ready to draw the swirls? Start by drawing a small circle in the middle of each lens. Then draw pairs of curved lines extending out from the center circle and reaching toward the edge of the lens.

6 The frames of Luna's Spectrespecs are decorated with stars and stardust. But you can decorate yours any way you like!

7 Spectrespecs are multicolored and sparkly, so get out your colors and get ready to see the magic!

TIME-TURNER

A Time-Turner is used to travel back in time. Hermione Granger used one to take extra classes in the third film! Do you wish you could use a Time-Turner to have even more time to draw? Try starting each drawing by practicing the hardest parts on scrap paper first to build your skills.

1 Start with a circle. If you want it to be super round, trace around the base of a cup or use a compass.

2 Draw two more circles around the first circle. Notice that the space between the circles is not even.

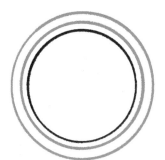

3 Draw two more circles around the outside of the first three. Pay attention to the space between each circle.

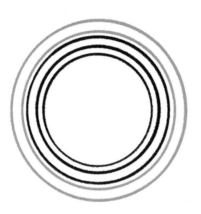

4 Draw two horizontal lines coming out of each side of the Time-Turner. (See how they appear in between circles?) At the end of each pair of lines, draw a half circle. Then, on top of the Time-Turner, draw two hooks using curved lines.

5 Now draw the details in the center of the Time-Turner. Start with an hourglass shape. Then draw four ovals on each side of it. Try tracing the pattern on scrap paper before adding it to your drawing.

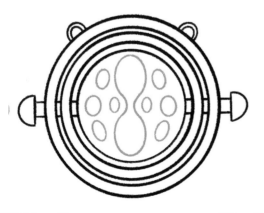

6 Draw a dashed line to start the Time-Turner's chain, going between the two hooks you drew in step four. Then use uneven dots and curved lines for the sand inside the hourglass.

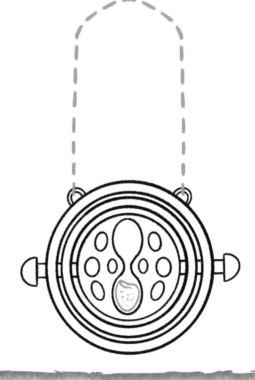

7 Draw a small rectangle between each dash you drew in step six.

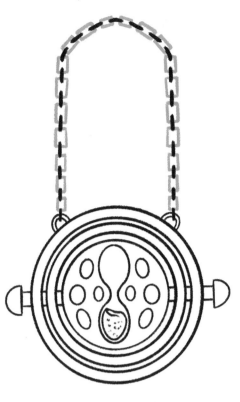

8 Congratulations, it's time to call this drawing done! What would you do if you had your own Time-Turner?

CHOCOLATE FROG BOX

Inside each Chocolate Frog box is a frog made of rich chocolate and a collectible card featuring a famous witch or wizard. For this drawing, you'll learn how to make a shape look three-dimensional instead of flat and how to decorate it. Ready to get started? Hop to it!

1 Start by drawing a pentagon, a shape with five equal sides. It should look like home base on a baseball field! If you are having a hard time getting the shape right, try tracing the one shown here or drawing five triangles that all meet in the middle.

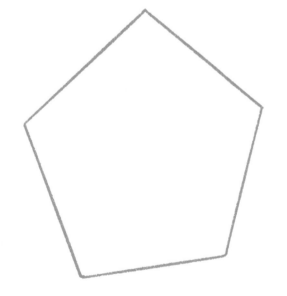

2 On the left side of the shape, draw two long, straight lines that run along the sides of the pentagon. Connect these lines to the pentagon with three short lines. These are the sides of the box.

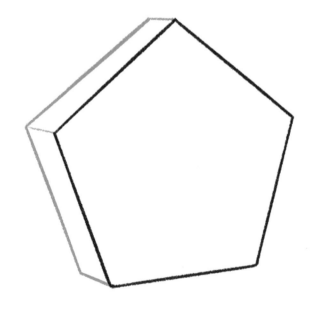

3 To make the lid of the box look 3-D instead of flat, draw a dot inside the pentagon as shown below. Then draw a line from each point of the pentagon to the dot.

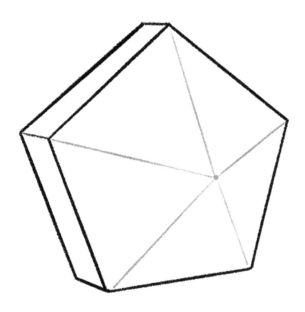

4 Time to start decorating! Draw an arc inside each triangle on the top of the box. Make sure all the arcs connect to make a flower shape. Then draw a row of smaller arcs on both sides of the box.

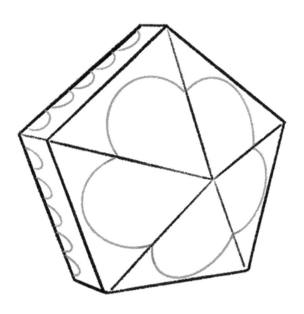

5 Draw an outline just inside the edge of your pentagon. Then draw an oval inside each of the five points. Using scalloped lines like the edges of a cloud, draw a fancy shape inside the flower you drew in step four.

6 Time for finishing touches! What colors will you make your box? And now that you can draw the box, try drawing a Chocolate Frog to go inside!

ARAGOG

This huge, talking spider (and former pet of Hagrid's) lives deep in the Forbidden Forest. When Ron and Harry faced Aragog in the second film, they were rescued by the Weasleys' enchanted Ford Anglia. But you won't need to be rescued from this drawing. You've got all the skills you need to draw the Acromantula—one hairy leg at a time!

1 Start by drawing the basic shape of the head. Then attach a curved line at the top for the body.

2 Use straight lines to sketch in six legs and curved lines for the two feelers. Pay attention to how many times each leg bends.

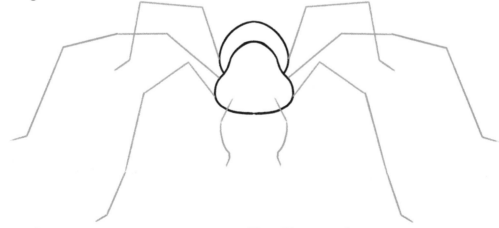

3 Draw a circle at each joint or bend in the legs and feelers.

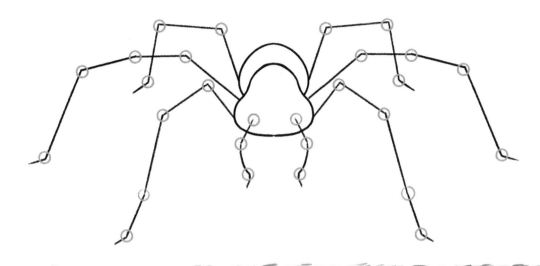

4 Make your spider's legs and feelers look 3-D by thickening up the outline around the lines and circles you drew in steps two and three. Keep the edges of the feet rounded. Then erase any lines you no longer need.

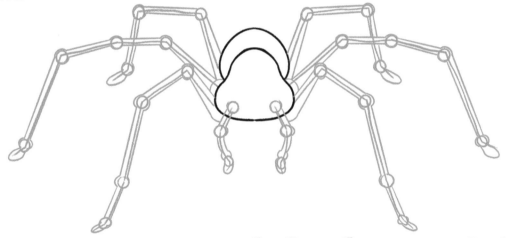

5 Redraw the outline of the head and body with curvy and jagged lines to make it look furry. Then draw the pincers on the face. Note the way they curve at the ends.

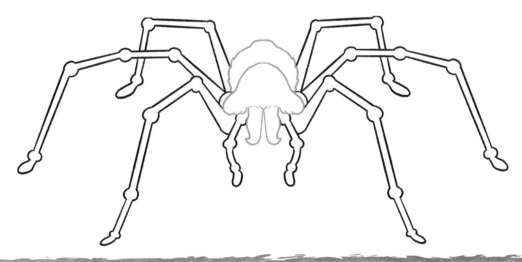

6 Draw the basic shapes of Araogog's many eyes. See how they're different sizes? Then use curved lines to draw the segments on the front of his body.

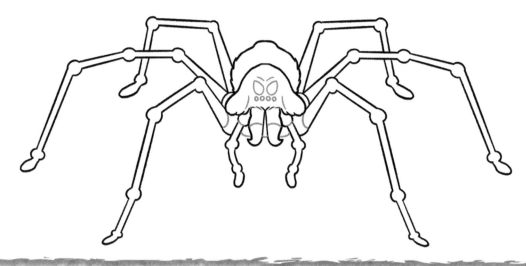

7 Use lots of short, curved lines to make the head, body, and joints look hairy. Then shade in the eyes leaving a tiny white highlight in each one.

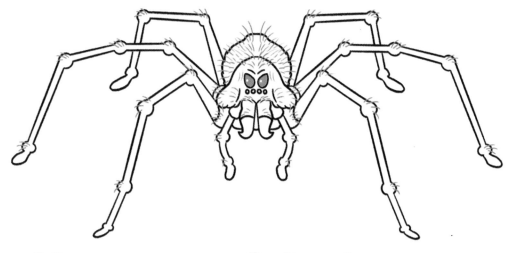

8 Use long, quick pencil lines to shade in your Aragog. Now that you can draw this Acromantula, try drawing him in the Forbidden Forest with the rest of his family!

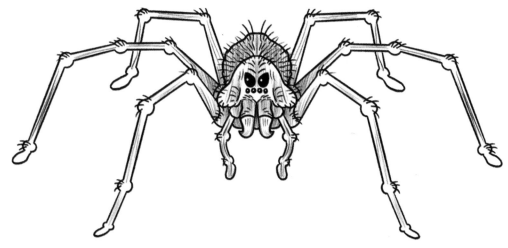

CROOKSHANKS

Crookshanks is a loyal and loving pet to Hermione. But the cat can be cranky around her friends and other pets, including Ron's pet rat, Scabbers. Luckily, there's no need for you to be cranky when learning to draw this clever cat. Big ovals and squiggly lines help give Crookshanks his fluffy appearance!

1 Draw a circle for the head. Then draw a long oval behind it for the body.

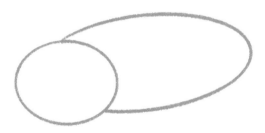

2 Finish drawing the cat's basic shape by adding straight lines for the arms, legs, and tail, kind of like a stick figure. Then draw ovals of different sizes for the paws.

3 Draw the outline of Crookshanks's body using squiggly lines for his fur. Notice that the squiggles get farther apart on his back and tail and closer together on his arms and face. Draw his paws using short, curved lines.

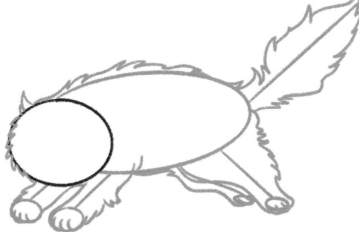

4 Use curved lines to draw the cat's fluffy shoulder and the top of his leg. Then used short curves to finish outlining his face and head. What kinds of lines will you use to draw the ear?

5 To make Crookshanks look extra furry, draw clusters of short, dashed lines all over his body. What do you notice about the direction of the lines in each cluster?

6 Break down the face into simple shapes. Each eye is a filled-in circle with a curved line on top. The snout is an upside-down "U," and the nose and mouth are two connected "V's." Don't forget the whiskers!

7 Double-check Crookshanks's proportions by making sure his head isn't too big or small for his body. Then clean up your outlines and start coloring this cat orange with brown stripes!

HEDWIG

Owls like Hedwig are the main way messages get delivered in the wizarding world. In the drawing world, you can deliver information through the shape of your lines. A curved line can make a wing that dips in or a head that juts out. A U-shaped line and a short dash can both look like feathers. How many different kinds of lines will you use in this drawing of Harry's snowy owl?

1 Start with a circle for the head. Then draw two curved guidelines inside the circle. These guidelines will help you draw a three-dimensional face and show which direction Hedwig is flying.

2 Sketch in the rest of the basic shapes that form Hedwig's body. Use half an oval for the body, two lines for the legs, and ovals for the feet.

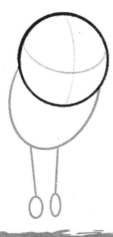

3 Draw the basic shapes of the wings and tail feathers. Use lots of big, curved lines. Notice where each new line connects to the body.

4 Redraw the outlines of the body to make Hedwig look more like an owl. Rows of U-shaped lines at the bottom of the wings look like feathers. Curved lines create Hedwig's wing bones, legs, and feet.

5 Draw tailfeathers by adding a row of "V's" along the bottom edge of the tail shape you drew in step three. Then draw straight lines between the tops of each "V" and the body.

6 Continue adding details to the feet and wings using curved lines and "U" shapes. For the face, draw ovals for eyes along the horizontal guideline and a diamond for the beak on the vertical guideline. Then erase the red guidelines.

7 Use different kinds of lines for the speckles on Hedwig's stomach and feathers on her head and face. Then draw a circle inside a circle in each eye. Leave the middle section of the eye white and fill in the rest.

8 Now finish off the details in the wings. Make sure to follow the curve of the wings as you draw. How many different kinds of lines will you use?

9 Complete your drawing by shading the tail feathers, tops of the legs, and the parts of the wings that dip in. Then color in Hedwig's yellow eyes and white feathers.

HIPPOGRIFF

This drawing is going to be legendary! These magical creatures (like Buckbeak, first seen in the third film) are half-eagle, half-horse. Drawing them is a great opportunity to work on texture. The eagle half of a Hippogriff's body is covered in feathers, while the coat on the horse-half is all hair. To show this contrast in textures, use lots of squiggly, scalloped, and curved lines on the front half and smooth lines on the back.

1 This magical creature starts with two circles for the body and an oval for the head. Connect the shapes with two straight guidelines that crisscross in in the middle of the left circle.

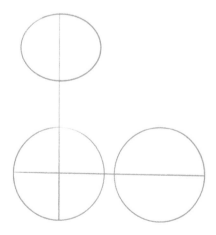

2 Use a squiggly line to connect the oval to the left circle. Then draw the eye and eyebrows. Use curved lines to draw the beak at the bottom right of the oval. Then draw a squiggly line for the neck.

3 Draw a leg at the bottom of each circle near the guidelines. Use squiggly lines for the belly and bird leg in the front and smooth lines for the horse leg in the back.

4 Draw the right legs peeking out from behind the body. Then draw the top of the wing using a long, curved line that extends out past the back of the body.

5 Draw the bottom of the wing using a scalloped line. When you're done, draw a hoof on the back leg and talons and claws on the front legs using long "U's" and curvy "V's."

6 Draw the horselike tail at the spot where the wing meets the leg using long, sweeping lines. Then draw the top of the right wing peeking out above the left one.

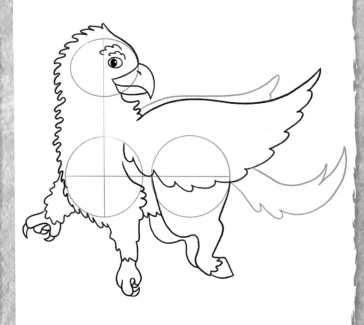

7 Time for texture! You can draw every feather on the wing or you can suggest lots of feathers by drawing three rows of connecting curves. Want a tip? Turn your paper sideways to draw them.

8 The feathers on the front half of the body stick up so they look more like clusters of lowercase "W's." Drawing the indication of a feather group here and there will trick the eye into seeing feathers all over!

9 Time for finishing touches. Erase any extra lines. Then add shading and hatch marks to give your Hippogriff more feathers and a three-dimensional feel. What colors will you use for your Hippogriff?

THESTRAL

Harry first meets a Thestral in the fifth film. These skeletal horses live in the Forbidden Forest and have reptilian faces and bat-like wings. They're normally only visible to people who've seen death—but no one will miss your drawing of this creature! Pay close attention to the subtle lines and details as you draw. How will you make your Thestral look one of a kind?

1 Start with the basic shapes—an oval for the head, a rectangle for the body, and a smaller oval for the hind end. Then connect the head and body with a straight line.

2 Use a combination of straight and curved lines to sketch in the wings, four legs, and tail.

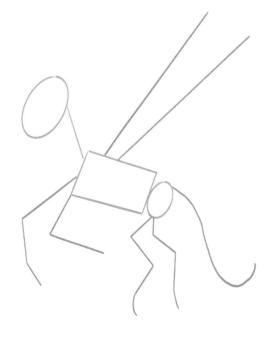

3 Use straight lines to block in the diamond shapes of the wings around the guidelines you drew in step two. See how the front wing hides part of the one behind it?

4 Draw the outline of the body around the stick figure Thestral from step three. Take it slow and pay attention to the different lines, like the curves around the face and the scalloped edges of the wings.

5 Add the eye by drawing three circles inside one another. Draw a triangular shape at each end. Then, add a brow line above the back triangle and curved lines for the nostril and cheekbone.

6 Use curves to add dips to the stomach, chest, and face, giving the Thestral its bony appearance. Then draw ridges along the spine and thorny details on the wings, snout, and ankles. Don't forget the mouth!

7 Use more curved lines to draw the ribs, knee-caps, and details in the hooves and neck. Then shade in the nostril and eye.

8 Use sweeping curved lines to sketch in the wing bones. Note that each line starts at the same spot and ends at a different point on the wing.

9 Double up the lines for the wing bones. Then add the bones that run along the top of each wing. Draw curved lines where the front wing meets the body.

10 You did it! Thestrals have smooth, dark skin. What materials will you use to make its skin look glossy and ghostly?

DOBBY

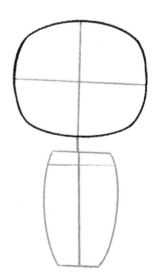

Dobby the house-elf may have started out with the Malfoy family, but he was most loyal to Harry Potter and his friends. That's because Harry always treated Dobby with kindness. He even tricked Lucius Malfoy into giving Dobby the sock that made him a free elf in the second film. What drawing tricks do you have up your sleeve?

1 Dobby's head starts as a rectangle with rounded corners. Divide it with two lines that crisscross in the center.

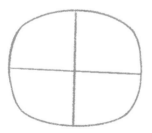

2 Draw a barrel shape for Dobby's body with a long, straight line at the top, a shorter straight line at the bottom, and curved lines on the sides. Then draw two straight guidelines that crisscross near the top.

3 Draw straight lines for the arms and legs and circles for the elbows. What shapes will you use for Dobby's feet?

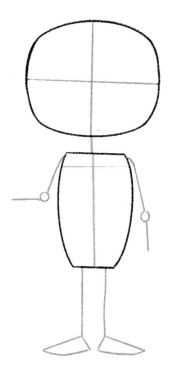

4 Sketch in the basic shapes of Dobby's hands. One looks like a diamond. The other starts with teardrop-shaped fingers. Use another curved line to start his sock.

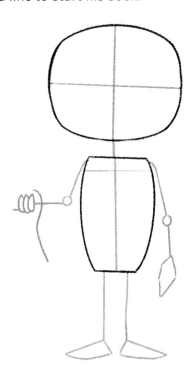

5 Draw the basic shapes of the ears. What do they remind you of? Then draw the outline of Dobby's body. His rag is boxy, but the lines in his arms, legs, fingers, and toes are curved. Don't forget his sock!

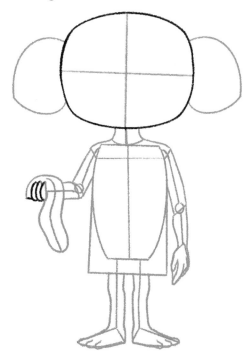

6 Draw two big circles for Dobby's eyes. Make sure the horizontal guideline runs right across the middle of them. Then sketch in the tie on his shoulder using jagged and curvy lines.

7 Redraw some of the outlines to give them more shape. Try using a mix of ragged and curved lines to make the rag look old and torn. Don't forget the wrinkles on his ears!

8 Fill in Dobby's eyes and draw the details on his face. It can be helpful to pick a starting point (like the nose) and then draw all the details around it. When you're finished, erase any leftover guidelines.

9 Add more details like the curved lines inside Dobby's ears, the stripes on his knees, and all the curved lines in the fabric of his clothes.

10 Erase any extra lines or smudges. Then step back and take a good look at your drawing? Where will you draw Dobby now that he's free of the Malfoys?

HOWLER

A Howler is a magical message that screams at you in the voice of the person who sent it. Poor Ron received one in the second film after his mom found out he and Harry took Mr. Weasley's flying car to Hogwarts. Luckily, no one is going to send you a Howler if you make a mistake while drawing one. After all, making mistakes is a great way to learn new drawing techniques!

1 Draw a square. Divide it into four equal sections with two lines that cross in the middle. These guidelines will help you with steps two and three!

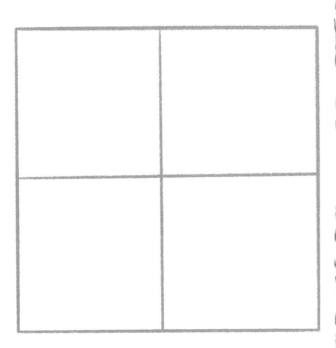

2 For the outline of the Howler, draw the straight lines in one section at a time. It may help to cover the other boxes with scrap paper as you work.

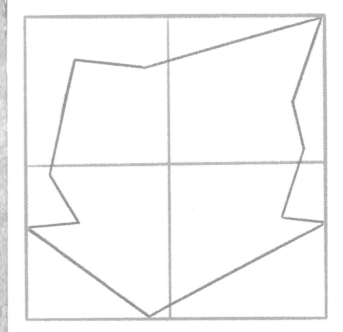

3 Time to start the folds of the Howler's mouth. Break down this step by drawing the straight and curved lines in one section at a time.

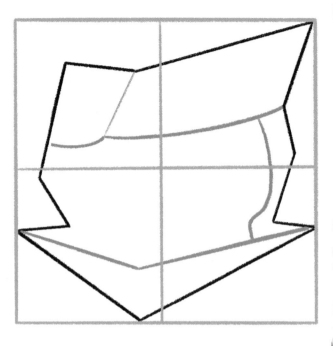

4 Draw the envelope flaps in the top two boxes. One looks like a crescent moon and the other like an upside-down "V." Draw two curved lines in the bottom boxes to connect the rest of the shapes.

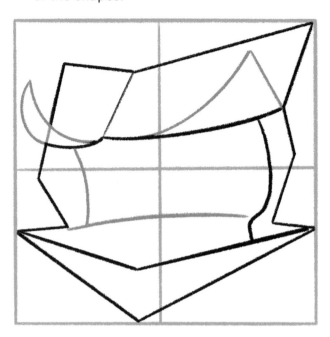

5 Draw rows of jagged teeth with lines that zigzag. Then draw a short, curved line above each flap near the top of the Howler. Erase the guidelines you drew in step one.

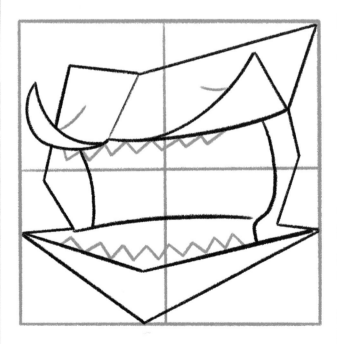

6 To make the teeth look 3-D, draw a short line coming down from each point of the zigzags you just drew. For the top teeth, connect those lines with another zigzag. On the bottom, connect them with a curve.

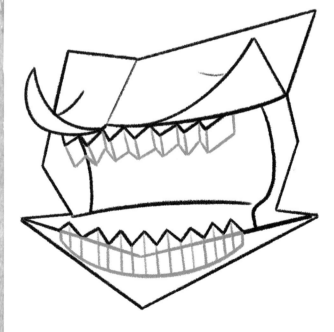

7 Draw a snakelike line for the tongue that dips down in the center. Then draw an upside-down "V" at one end and a short, straight line at the other end.

8 Draw two more curved lines to connect the shapes in the tongue. Then add some quick detail lines at the back of the Howler.

9 Shade in the shadowy parts of the Howler. Then color the envelope red. What will your first howling message say—and who will you send it to?

MONSTER BOOK OF MONSTERS

The Monster Book of Monsters bites! Luckily, Hagrid shows his Care of Magical Creatures class a trick for opening the book in the third film: if you stroke its spine, the book will open right up! If this drawing makes you feel like you might snap, try taking a break. Going for a walk, drinking some water, or just leaving the room and coming back later can help you think of solutions to your drawing dilemmas!

1 Start by drawing a long, skinny rectangle that tilts a little. Then draw two angled lines coming out of the top corners. Connect those lines with another straight line to form a box shape.

2 The top of the box is furry, so use a combination of squiggly lines and loose "V" and "W" shapes to show the hair. Make sure to leave a part in the front for the mouth.

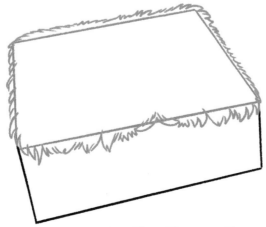

3 Draw a long, curved tentacle on either side of the part you drew in step two. Then draw three smaller tentacles on each side.

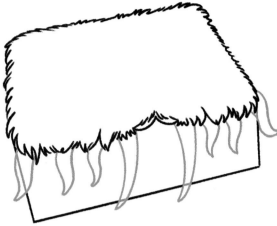

4 Time for teeth! Start drawing the book's mouth by adding a row of small teeth between the tentacles you drew in step three. Start with five curvy vertical lines. Between each pair of lines, draw an upside-down triangle.

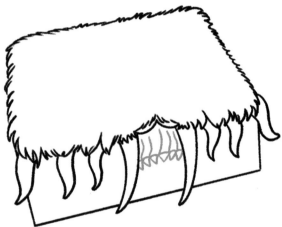

5 For the eyes, start with a five-sided pentagon. The point of the pentagon should touch the part above the mouth. Draw a curved line to divide the shape. Then draw four circles above the curve.

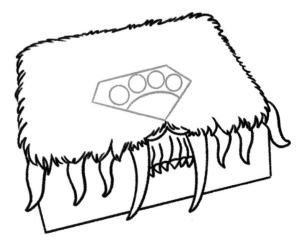

6 Use short, curved lines to make the edges of the pentagon look hairy. Then draw a squiggly line above the circles. Draw the nose below the curve using more curved lines and shading. Erase the red lines.

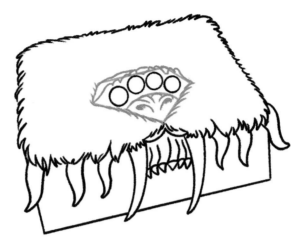

7 Draw five curvy tentacles on the bottom just like you did in step three, leaving a space on one side for the tongue. Then draw a half moon below the mouth. Add more teardrop-shaped teeth along the curve.

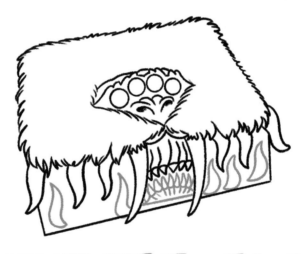

8 Look closely at the drawing below. What kinds of lines will you use to make the bottom of the book look furry? What kinds of lines will show a hint of the pages behind the tentacles?

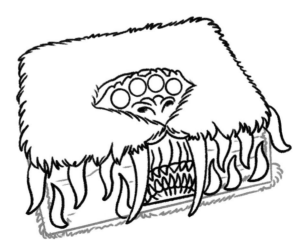

9 Use curving lines to draw a forked tongue in the space between the tentacles. Erase any furry lines it overlaps. Then fill in the eyes leaving white highlights in the same spot on each eye.

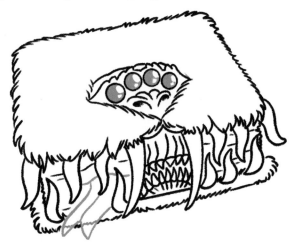

10 Use tiny clusters of short lines to create the texture of hair. Some of the lines look like "W" shapes. Others are short dashes.

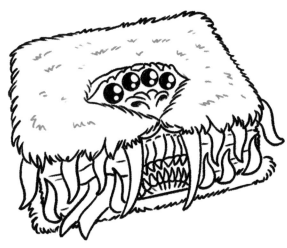

11 Get ready to read! Clean up any smudges and trace over the outlines using a thin black marker. What colors will you use to bring this book to life?

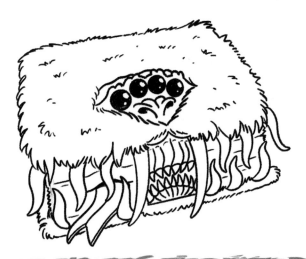

GRYFFINDOR CREST

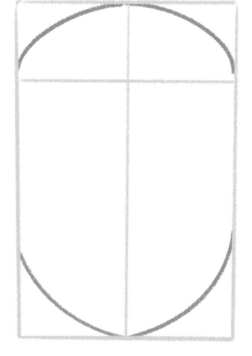

Gryffindors like Harry, Ron, and Hermione are known for their courage, bravery, and determination. Are you feeling brave enough tackle all the straight lines and right angles in this crest? Here are some tips for drawing straight lines: Fold your paper into four sections and let the creases guide you. Or try using a tool like a ruler, straight edge, or the corner of a book or box as a guide.

1 Start by drawing a tall rectangle. Then divide it into two small rectangles at the top and two long rectangles at the bottom. These guide-lines will help you draw the outline of the crest.

2 Draw a curved line inside each smaller rectangle.

3 Reshape the top of the crest using curved lines. Try to make the lines on the right and left sides the same.

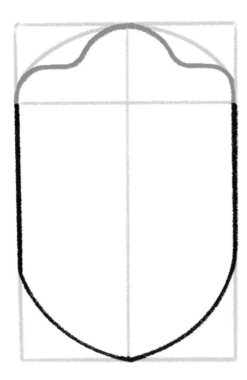

4 Double-up the outline of the crest to make it look like a frame. Then erase the guidelines you drew in steps one and two.

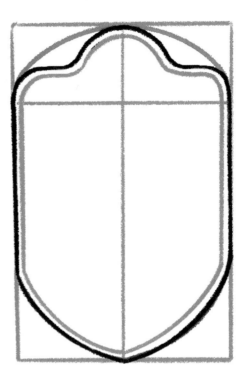

5 You did it! You'll use this crest to draw each of the house crests on pages 50, 60, and 62, as well.

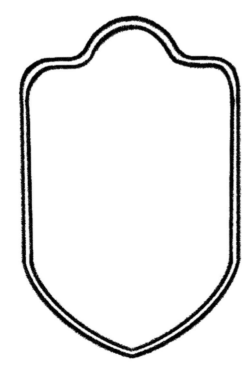

6 For the Gryffindor house crest, draw a stick figure lion inside your outline from step five. The head is a trapezoid, and the body has two ovals. Straight lines connect the shapes.

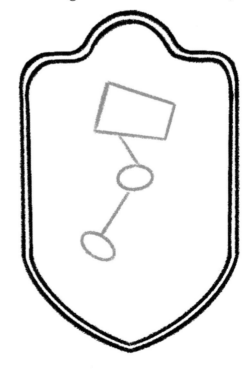

7 Use curved lines to lightly sketch in the arms, legs, and tail. Think of this stick figure as the skeleton of your lion.

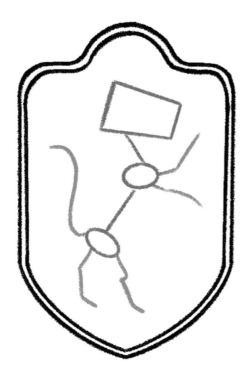

8 Draw the outline of the lion around the stick figure you just drew and add a triangle at the end of the tail. Then erase any lines you no longer need.

9 Round out the edges of the lion. Draw the eye and roaring mouth. Use jagged lines for the hair on the tail and mane.

10 Draw the guidelines for the letter "G" in the lower right-hand part of the crest. Start with a square. Then divide it into four equal sections.

11 Draw a fancy capital "G" inside the box from step ten. To make it easier, draw the lines inside one box at a time. When you're done, erase the guidelines.

12 Your bravery has paid off! Finish up the Gryffindor crest by adding the house colors of red and gold. Then try drawing it on a scarf for Harry, Hermione, or Ron!

SLYTHERIN CREST

Slytherins like Draco Malfoy are known for their pride, cunning, and ambition. Do you want to draw a Slytherin crest to be proud of? Here's a tip: Try not to grip your pencil too tightly. A tight hold makes it harder to draw all the sweeping curves in the Slytherin snake. Practice drawing curves on scrap paper until you start to feel the difference! Then flip to pages 54–55 for instructions on how to draw the crest outline.

1 Draw an oval in the middle of your crest. Then divide the oval into sections using vertical and horizontal sections. The top sections should be bigger than the others.

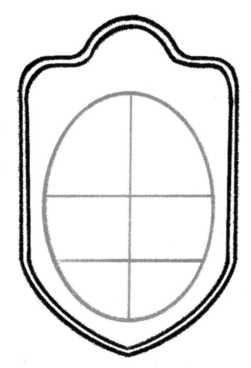

2 Starting in the upper left section, draw the spine of the snake. This curvy line runs down the left side of the crest, sweeps along the bottom, loops in the middle, and tapers off back at the top.

3 Draw the outline of the body around the spine you drew in step two. The lines will overlap in the middle section where the body coils. Once you're done, erase the red guidelines.

4 Draw an eye, a curved line for the mouth, and a forked tongue. Then draw a box in the upper right-hand part of the crest. Divide it into four sections with two straight lines that crisscross.

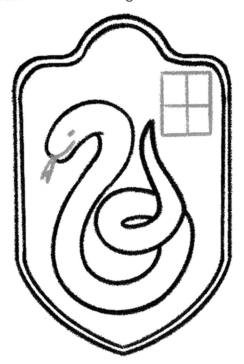

5 Draw the "S" for Slytherin inside your guidelines from step four. You can focus on one section at a time or draw the "S" as a whole. Erase your guidelines when you're done.

6 The Slytherin crest shimmers in shades of green and silver. Try using your pencils or markers to make this house crest shine!

RAVENCLAW CREST

The students in Ravenclaw house at Hogwarts are known for their wit, wisdom, and love of learning. The house was founded by Rowena Ravenclaw, and Luna Lovegood is one of its many students. To draw the Ravenclaw house crest, start by following steps 1–5 on pages 54–55 for the crest's basic shape. Then take out your pencil and get ready to draw the house's signature animal, the raven!

1 Draw a circle for the raven's head inside your crest. Attach an almost-oval for the body. Then draw two lines coming from the top of the oval for the wings.

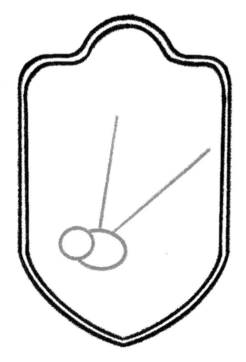

2 Block in the rest of the bird's basic shapes. The right wing and tail look like a blocky letter "L." The left wing gets tucked behind them. Use triangles for the beak and legs.

3 Reshape the outline so your drawing looks more like a bird. Use squiggly lines around the wings for feathers and curved lines for the claws, beak, and head. Then erase any lines you no longer need.

4 Draw a small rectangle in the upper left-hand part of the crest. Then divide it into four sections. These guidelines will help you draw the "R" for Ravenclaw!

5 Draw a fancy capital "R" inside the box from step four. You can draw it all at once or draw lines inside one section at a time. When you're done, erase the red guidelines.

6 Time for color! The Ravenclaw house colors are blue and silver. If you don't have a silver pencil, use your Ravenclaw smarts to mix the colors you do have to see what works best!

HUFFLEPUFF CREST

Do you value dedication, patience, and loyalty? If so, you would probably get along with Hufflepuffs like Cedric Diggory and Justin Finch-Fletchley! Your good nature will serve you well as you draw the Hufflepuff badger and continue to develop your drawing skills. But first, start by drawing the outline of the house crest from pages 54-55.

1 Start by drawing a stick figure badger. Use a large oval for the head and two smaller ovals for the body. Connect the ovals with curved lines for the spine.

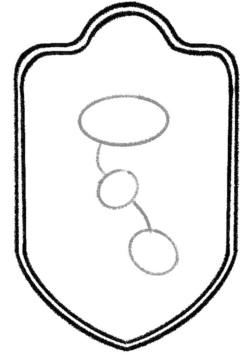

2 Add more lines for the arms, legs, and tail.

3 Draw the outline of the badger around your stick figure using straight lines. Keep your lines light and loose. Then erase the guidelines from steps one and two.

4 Now, round out the edges and blocky lines of the badger. Use some jagged lines to show the claws, tail, and patches of fur. Don't forget to add the eye!

5 Draw the guidelines for the Hufflepuff "H" in the top right of your crest. Start by drawing a square, then divide it into four sections with crisscrossing lines.

6 Draw a fancy letter "H" inside the box from step five. You can draw it section by section or all at once. Then erase the guidelines.

7 Color your crest with Hufflepuff's classic yellow and black. How will you show off your coloring skills?

HARRY POTTER

Are you ready to draw the most famous young wizard at Hogwarts? Here's a magical secret: All the drawings of people in this book start out the same way—with a *stick figure*! Starting with a stick figure helps you capture the person's position before you add details. Harry may be standing still in this drawing, but you'll be able to use this same technique to draw wizards in any pose—running, flying, or casting a spell!

1 Draw an oval for the head. Divide it with two curved lines that crisscross right below the center. Draw the shield-like shape of the torso below the head, with a slightly curved spine inside.

2 Sketch in the arms, legs, and triangular feet as if you were drawing a stick figure. Then draw circles at the joints (shoulders, elbows, wrists, knees, and ankles). Harry's hands are in his pockets, so his arms are bent.

3 Draw a halo around Harry's head for hair and two circles for eyes. See how the eyes rest on the horizontal guideline? Then use a combination of ovals and straight lines to thicken the arms, legs, and neck.

4 Once you have the frame of the body, you can draw the outline of Harry's pants, robe, and the neck of his sweater. Then use lots of "V" shapes for the messy fringe of Harry's hair.

5 For Harry's eyes, start by drawing two smaller circles inside your circles from step three. Then draw a horizontal line through each eye. The eyelids and brows are shaped like crescent moons. Finish off the face with his mouth, nose, and lightning-bolt scar!

TURN TO PAGE 6 FOR A CLOSER LOOK AT HARRY'S EYES!

6 Lines are magical! Straight lines form a "V" for Harry's sleeve. Short, curved lines branching out from the inner elbow show the folds in the top half of his robe. Additional curved lines add shagginess to his hair.

7 Build up the details of Harry's clothes using curved lines and tiny hatch marks. Then shade in the top half of his eyes, leaving the tiniest circles white. Harry's glasses are two large circles connected by one short line.

8 You drew Harry Potter! Clean up your drawing by erasing any smudges and extra lines. If you like, trace over the outlines with a thin black marker. Then grab your Gryffindor red and gold and get ready to color!

RON WEASLEY

It's time to draw Harry's loyal, brave, and funny best friend, Ron Weasley. There are a lot of similarities between the drawings of Ron and Harry in this book—*and* a lot of differences. Just like their personalities! You may want to flip to other character drawings as you work. Comparing two drawings is a great way to learn!

1 Start by drawing an oval for Ron's head and a shield-like torso. Then add curved guidelines for the face and spine. Note that the shape of Ron's torso has slightly rounded edges.

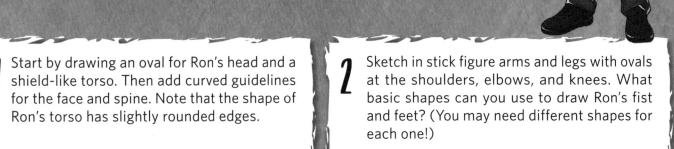

2 Sketch in stick figure arms and legs with ovals at the shoulders, elbows, and knees. What basic shapes can you use to draw Ron's fist and feet? (You may need different shapes for each one!)

3 Use ovals and straight lines to thicken Ron's arms, legs, and neck. Then add a circle for each eye and a halo for hair. Draw a capital "T" inside his fist to create a thumb. Then erase your stick figure guidelines.

4 Reshape the outline from step three so it looks like Ron is wearing pants, a sweater, and shoes. For the ear, draw a half-moon with a curve inside. And use lots of messy "V" shapes for his hair.

5 Time to draw the face! Flip back to page 6 for tips on drawing eyes. See how Ron's eyebrows tilt up in the center? Don't forget to draw the freckles above Ron's nose!

6 Shade in the upper part of Ron's eyes. Then add details to his hair and clothes. Curved lines create a collar and messy hair. Straight lines trim his sweater. Use diagonal lines for his pants and tie.

7 Clean up the outlines and erase any smudges and guidelines you don't need. Then color in Ron's signature red Weasley hair. What magical adventures will you draw Ron into next?

HERMIONE GRANGER

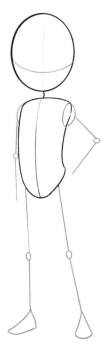

Hermione Granger is top of her class and a top-notch friend to Harry and Ron throughout the Harry Potter films. But even Hermione makes mistakes while learning new spells. Is it hard to start a new drawing because you feel like it has to be perfect? Make a bunch of super-messy Hermione drawings on scrap paper before you begin to shake off that feeling. The messier the better!

1 Draw an oval for Hermione's head and guide-lines on her face. Her body is turned, so the curved line on one side of her torso should be longer than the other. Then draw an oval for her shoulder.

2 Add curved lines at her shoulders. Then draw stick arms and legs and ovals for her elbows and knees. See how one arm bends at the elbow? What shapes will you use to draw the feet?

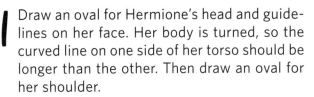

3 Draw two circles for eyes. They sit on the curved guideline you drew in step one. Then sketch in the basic shapes of her hair.

4 Thicken the outline of her body using a combination of straight and curved lines. See the sideways "V" at her bent elbow and the "W" in the hand that rests on her hip? Erase the old guidelines.

5 Draw the outlines of Hermione's hair and clothes. Her bangs are made up of ragged "W" and "V" shapes, but the lines of her curls are softer and wavier. Erase any lines you no longer need.

6 Time to draw Hermione's face! For tips on drawing eyes, flip back to page 6. For her skirt, draw a curve above each knee and long, straight lines on either side for pleats.

7 How many different "V" shapes do you see in Hermione's collar, tie, and sweater? Use them to help you draw the details in her outfit.

8 Add shading to the top half of each eye and to Hermione's eyelids. Then add details to her hair. Notice the way the curved lines in her waves connect to one another.

9 Add final details like the curved lines on Hermione's shoulder and the spot where her arm bends. Draw short dashed lines on the waistband and cuff of her sweater.

10 Clean up your drawing and trace over the outlines with a thin black marker. Then add color! What magical adventures will you draw Hermione into first?

DRACO MALFOY

Draco Malfoy is known for doing whatever it takes to get what he wants. And unlike Harry, he *wanted* to be sorted into Slytherin! In a drawing you can use details like a sneering mouth instead of a smile to tell a story about someone's personality. What do the other details in this drawing reveal about Harry Potter's biggest rival at Hogwarts?

1 Draw the basic shapes and guidelines of the head and body. Draco's body faces a different direction than his head. To make this easier to see, draw his spine closer to one side of his torso than the other.

2 Draw an oval at his shoulder. Then draw stick figure arms and legs. Add triangles for the hands and feet and smaller ovals for the elbows and knees. Notice that Draco's legs are longer than his torso.

3 Draw Draco's neck. Then add two circles for eyes on the horizontal guideline. Next, draw a halo around his head for hair.

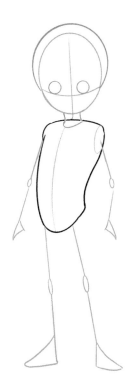

4 Using straight and curved lines, draw the shapes of Draco's arms and legs around the stick figure you drew in step two. For his hands, draw his thumbs and pointer fingers around the tips of the triangles.

5 Ready to add another layer to your drawing? Draw the outline of Draco's pants, shoes, and wizarding robe. What shapes do you see that might help you?

6 Draw two half-moon ears. Notice that they are slightly lower than his eyes. Then use short, curved lines to frame Draco's face. Use more curved lines on the outer edge of his hair to make it look slicked back.

7 For Draco's eyes, follow the tips on page 6. His eyelids are rounded but his eyebrows are straight and pointed. So is his mouth! Then erase all your leftover guidelines.

8 To finish Draco's face, fill in the parts of his eyes that are shaded in the book. Now, add final detail lines to his hair.

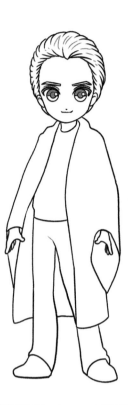

9 Finish up the details in Malfoy's clothes. Curved lines on his pants and robe make them look flowy. Dashes add texture to his sweater and "V" shapes and diagonal lines form his collar and tie.

10 Erase any smudges and extra lines. Trace over the final outline with a thin black marker. Finish up by coloring his sweater and tie in Slytherin green and silver!

LUNA LOVEGOOD

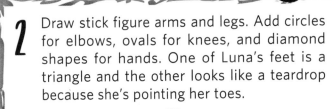

When Harry meets Luna Lovegood in the fifth film, he first notices her dreamy look and limitless imagination. But soon he learns she's a great friend too! Luna Lovegood is the Hogwarts student most likely to believe in the impossible—especially if she reads about it in the pages of the *Quibbler*! What possibilities do you see in this drawing of Luna? Pick up your pencil and find out!

1
Draw an oval head and a rectangular body that squishes in at the middle. Then draw a straight line from the top of her head to the bottom of her body. Add a curved guideline for her face.

2
Draw stick figure arms and legs. Add circles for elbows, ovals for knees, and diamond shapes for hands. One of Luna's feet is a triangle and the other looks like a teardrop because she's pointing her toes.

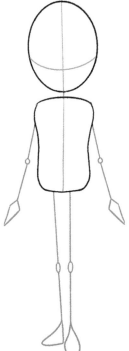

3 Thicken the outlines of her arms and legs. Notice how they are wider at the tops than they are at the bottoms. Then draw Luna's hands. Try tracing them on scrap paper first to practice.

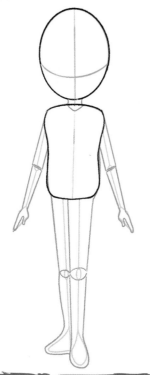

4 Draw a circle for each eye on the horizontal guideline you drew in step one. Then draw Luna's hair using long, wavy lines. Notice how high her hair comes above the oval of her head.

5 Draw a wave like an upside-down "U" for Luna's bangs. See where it crosses the guidelines you drew in step one? Then draw her robe, the deep "V" of her sweater, and the wavy bottom of her skirt.

6 Draw a dark circle in each eye along with a smaller, circular highlight. Draw half-moons for eyelids and attach eyelashes. Notice that her eyebrows rest high on her forehead giving Luna a dreamy look. Erase any red lines.

7 Draw tiny curves for ears and diamond shapes for earrings. Shade in the top half of each eye. Then use long, curvy lines to make her hair look extra wavy. The lines should move in the direction her hair flows.

8 Add finishing touches! Use dashes for Luna's knees and curved lines for the folds in her robes and details on her shoes. Straight lines form pleats on her skirt and stripes in her tie. An upside-down "V" shapes her collar.

9 Ready to add color? Luna has pale blue eyes and white-blonde hair. Try drawing her making friends with a magical creature or watching the world through her Spectrespecs!

ALBUS DUMBLEDORE

When Harry Potter has a problem or feels stuck in the films, he often goes to Professor Dumbledore for advice. Are you feeling stuck on a drawing? Try taping it to the wall, taking a giant step back, and looking at it from a distance. Or turn your paper upside down! Sometimes you have to look at your drawing from a different perspective before you can figure out what to do next.

1 Start with a circle for the head. Divide it into to four equal sections with two straight, crisscrossing lines. Below the head, draw a shape that looks like home base in baseball. Connect the two shapes with a short line.

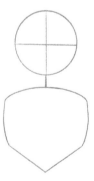

2 Draw two straight lines from the bottom of the torso to where the feet will be. Then sketch in the basic shapes of the arms and hands. One hand is a rectangle. The other is a loose "W" shape.

3 Sketch the outline of Dumbledore's body using straight, wavy, and curved lines. Include his hair, beard, and robes. Then draw ovals for eyes on the middle guidelines.

4 Use lines to add detail to your drawing. When you make the outline of Dumbledore's face curvier, his skin will look wrinkly. A combination of curved and straight lines will make his robes look flowy.

5 Use curved lines to finish the hat. Then use your guidelines to draw the face. Draw the eyebrows and eyelids in the top half of the circle and the mouth, nose, and glasses in the bottom. Erase extra lines.

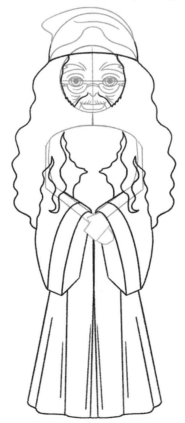

6 Draw fingers using "U" shapes and wavy lines. Use more wavy lines to add details to Dumbledore's beard. Do you see the way it's tied above his hands?

7 Add shading to Dumbledore's eyebrows, beard, hat, and robes. Then decorate his hat with stars and color in his robes. What advice do you imagine he wants to give Harry Potter?

HOGWARTS EXPRESS

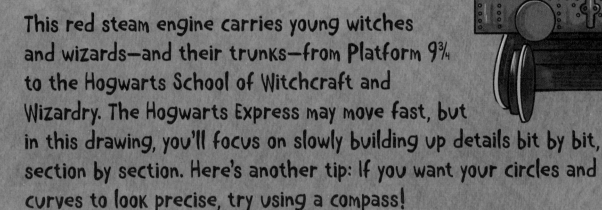

This red steam engine carries young witches and wizards—and their trunks—from Platform 9¾ to the Hogwarts School of Witchcraft and Wizardry. The Hogwarts Express may move fast, but in this drawing, you'll focus on slowly building up details bit by bit, section by section. Here's another tip: If you want your circles and curves to look precise, try using a compass!

1 Start with a circle. Then draw a long, skinny rectangle below it. Connect the shapes with two equal, angled lines.

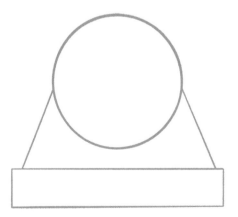

2 Keep drawing basic shapes, including two smaller circles, a medium-sized circle, and another, smaller rectangle. Pay close attention to their size and placement.

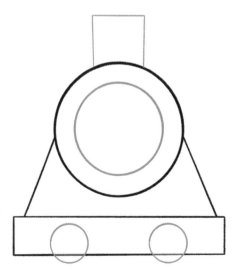

3 Draw a tall, skinny oval under each of the smaller circles you drew in step two. Then connect them with two horizontal lines.

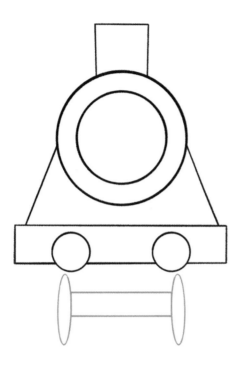

4 Use straight and curved lines to finish the details in the wheels. Follow the outer edges of the skinny ovals you drew in step three to get the curves just right.

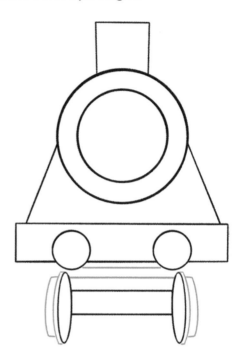

5 Use long, curved lines to connect the bottom of the train to the wheels. Then draw two curvy shapes at the top of the train to create a smokestack.

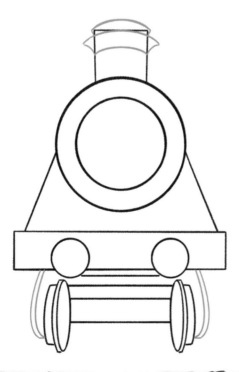

6 Start adding the details on the train using a combination of straight and curved lines and simple shapes like circles and rectangles. How will you draw the detail on the smokestack?

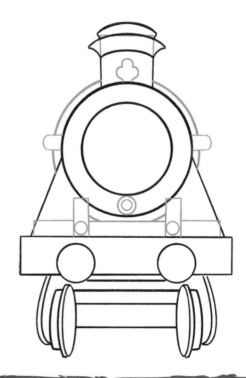

7 Draw two rectangles on the front of the train. Then draw a curved plaque above it. Add some gears around these two shapes. Look for circles, squares, and arcs to help you simplify them.

8 Keep adding details to the front of the train, bit by bit! How will you break each gear down into basic lines and shapes?

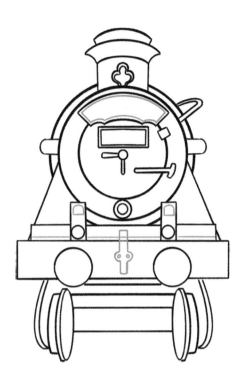

9 Write the identification number and the words "Hogwarts Express" on the two plaques on the front of the train. Then draw circles for bolts all over the train.

10 This steam engine is red, but what colors will you make the gears? Now that you can draw the Hogwarts Express, try drawing it zipping toward Hogwarts!

HOGWARTS CREST

The Hogwarts crest has four sections—one for each of the four Hogwarts houses: Gryffindor, Ravenclaw, Slytherin, and Hufflepuff. Once you've mastered drawing the crest for each house, you'll be ready to put them together into the Hogwarts crest. You'll use plenty of grids and guidelines to help you along the way!

1 Start by drawing a square. Then divide it into four sections. The two bottom sections should be slightly taller than the two top sections.

2 Draw the outline of the crest. Focus on drawing the lines inside one box at a time. Notice how they connect to the lines in the boxes next to them.

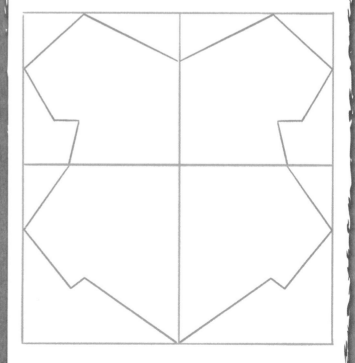

3 Refine the outline of the crest, continuing to work on one box at a time. Use curved lines and arches to make the top corners of the crest bend backward.

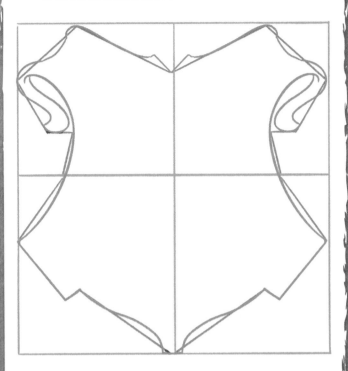

4 To create the decorative trim, draw lines that run parallel to the outlines of the crest. Don't forget to outline the guidelines in the middle too.

5 Draw the Gryffindor lion and Slytherin snake in the top sections of the crest and the Hufflepuff badger and Ravenclaw raven in the bottom sections. Flip to pages 55, 58, 60, and 62 for instructions!

6 Draw a square in the middle of the crest. Then draw a cross through the center of it. These guidelines will help you draw the "H" for Hogwarts!

7 Draw a curve inside each side of the square. Connect the curves by drawing a short, straight line in each corner.

8 Draw the outline of a letter "H" in the center of the square. Then erase any extra lines inside the square (including parts of the animals you drew in step five).

9 Use short, curved lines and dashes inside the crest's trim and the center section to make the crest look fancy and shiny. Follow the curves of the outline as you draw.

10 Time for color! Remember to use the different house colors in each section. Now that you can draw the Hogwarts crest, try drawing it big on poster paper to hang in your room!

HOGWARTS CASTLE

Hogwarts castle is the home of Hogwarts School of Witchcraft and Wizardry—and the place where all the magic happens! From the Great Hall to the Astronomy Tower, this campus is famous for teaching magic, building friendships, and holding secrets. Want to know a secret about this drawing? Every building, tower, and aqueduct starts with a rectangle!

1 Draw a long rectangle. Then divide it into three uneven sections. The middle section should be the smallest.

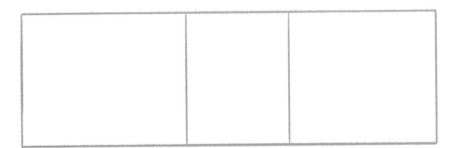

2 Start adding rectangles in each section for the buildings, towers, and turrets. Focus on one section at a time. What do you notice about the size of each rectangle and where it's placed?

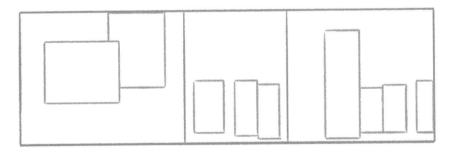

3 Draw more rectangles around the ones you drew in step two. Some will overlap a little with other rectangles. Use the drawing below to help you place each new shape.

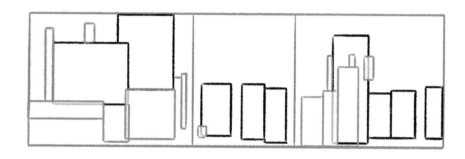

4 Use upside-down "V's" to add pointed roofs to all the towers and turrets. Wondering which rectangles are meant to be towers? Peek ahead to the final drawing for clues!

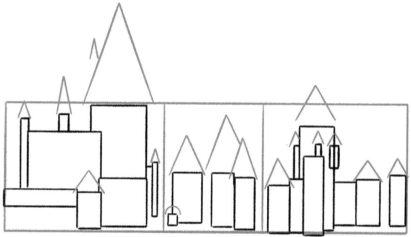

5 Draw a curved line at the bottom of each "V" from step four. Then use angled lines for the rest of the rooftops. Erase the lines below each tower and other marks you don't need.

6 Draw angled lines beneath the castle to sketch in where the rocky cliffs will go. Then add four straight lines below the middle towers for the aqueduct.

7 Redraw the lines below the castle so they look rocky and uneven. Then draw the arches in the aqueduct and erase any guidelines you no longer need.

8 Time to draw details on the Great Hall, tower roofs, and aqueduct! You'll use lots of straight lines, arches, and ovals. Add a curved line inside each arch in the aqueduct to make it look more 3-D.

9 Use rectangles and circles to add windows to the rest of the buildings and towers. Notice that the windows on the tower roofs get smaller as they go up.

10 Use a combination of uneven lines, dots, and dashes to create the rocky texture of the mountain. Most of the lines point up to form peaks, but the shapes under the Great Hall point downward instead.

11 Clean up your outlines and erase any messy lines or smudges. Color the windows with yellows and oranges to create a glow from inside. Shade in the dark walls last to avoid smudging!

THE KNIGHT BUS

The Knight Bus that Harry rides in the third film is known for driving fast! Drawing the Knight Bus won't be quite as quick as Harry's ride to Diagon Alley, but you can get yourself ready by tracing the bus in the book and by drawing lots of boxes on scrap paper before you begin. Steps one and two show you how to do it!

1 Draw a tall rectangle. To the left of it, draw a bigger rectangle—make sure the top and bottom angle outward.

2 Draw a straight line between the top right corners of each shape. Then draw a line between the top left corners, the bottom right corners, and the bottom left corners. Your lines will overlap in spots!

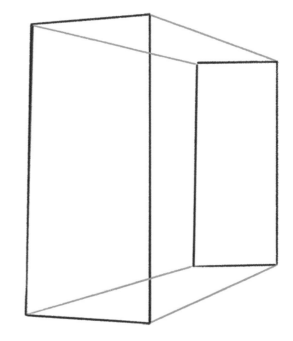

3 Round out the outline of the box to make it look more like a triple-decker bus. Make sure to leave two half-moon openings at the bottom for the tires.

4 Sketch in two ovals and a half-moon for the tires. (The fourth tire is hidden.) Then draw a rectangular shape on the front of the bus. See how it's wider at the top?

5 Draw a smaller oval inside each tire. Then use curved lines to make the tires look 3-D. Now add details to the grille and a platform to the back of the bus.

6 Draw a short, horizontal line on the front of the bus and a longer one on the side. (They should be parallel to the bottom edges of your box from step two.) Then draw a dashed vertical line where the horizontal lines meet.

7 First, draw three vertical lines at the front of the bus, parallel to the lines from your box from step two. Pay attention to their length and placement. Connect them with angled lines on the top and bottom.

8 Use rectangles to block in the bus's windows. Keep using the guidelines from step two to get the angles right.

9 Using the rectangles you drew in step eight as a guide, draw individual windows with vertical sides and rounded corners. Then erase the box you drew in steps one and two.

10 Take a close look at the details in this step. What basic shapes and lines do you see? What strategies can you use to draw the curves on the hood at the proper angles?

11 Write the words "Knight Bus" on the front of the bus. Then use straight lines to add details and trim. Notice the way the lines on the side of the bus get closer together as they move farther away.

12 Ready to add color and send this bus on magical adventures? Who is getting on this magical purple bus? Where is it heading? What adventures await?